Henry Attwell

Manual of General History

SALZWASSER
VERLAG

Henry Attwell

Manual of General History

Reprint of the original, first published in 1859.

1st Edition 2022 | ISBN: 978-3-37513-300-9

Verlag (Publisher): Salzwasser Verlag GmbH, Zeilweg 44, 60439 Frankfurt, Deutschland
Vertretungsberechtigt (Authorized to represent): E. Roepke, Zeilweg 44, 60439 Frankfurt, Deutschland
Druck (Print): Books on Demand GmbH, In de Tarpen 42, 22848 Norderstedt, Deutschland

MANUAL

OF

GENERAL HISTORY

FOR THE USE OF SCHOOLS.

TRANSLATED FROM THE NOORTHEY COURSE

BY

PROFESSOR HENRY ATTWELL, K.O.C.

M.C.P. ETC.

LONDON

LONGMAN, GREEN, LONGMAN, AND ROBERTS

1859

INTRODUCTION.

THIS book is a translation of an unpublished Manual used in the excellent school of Noorthey, Holland, and was prepared for the use of the pupils of that institution. My object in translating and publishing it is to supply the want of a faithful outline of general history which can be filled up according to the capacities of learners.

The Manual has been for many years successfully employed in the above school in teaching boys of from ten to seventeen years old; alterations and additions have been made from time to time until it has become, to my thinking, as nearly perfect, of its kind, as possible.

To speak so highly in praise of such a common-place looking little book will not seem singular to those who know how inferior most of our elementary school books are, and especially those abridgments and catechisms which, possessing only the questionable recommendation of being calculated to save teacher and pupil trouble, are still in extensive use.

As this Manual of Universal History differs in form from most English school books, I may, perhaps, be allowed to suggest the way in which I consider it may be employed to the greatest advantage.

The text should be committed to memory, little by little, by the pupil; but not until it has been made palatable and easy of digestion.

Sometimes a line, sometimes a single name and date, will be sufficient; but it will be well, in the case of beginners, never to learn by heart any part of the text before the oral lesson has been given.

The meaning of every difficult word and construction should be carefully explained, so that the pupil may feel that what he learns is an exact summing up of what has been conveyed to him by word of mouth.

Before a fresh lesson is begun, as much of the preceding parts as relates immediately to the period under consideration should be re-said.

No new NAMES should be introduced until the course has been gone through once at least.

If a boy learn the text with difficulty and dislike, we must, in most cases, conclude that our preliminary oral teaching has been faulty.

" LYCURGUS " [880] will not be a hard name and date to a boy who has taken an interest in the black broth, and the iron money, and the young Spartans' orchard adventures and table-talk.

But though it is of so much importance to excite and sustain interest, care should be taken not to overcrowd a lesson with illustration. A good teacher will know, within a little, what he means to say before he confronts his class, and will be careful not to let a forward pupil lead him into digressions which will spoil the *ensemble* of his lesson.

In teaching beginners, a large map is preferable to an atlas, and a black board and chalk should be constantly in readiness.

In going through the course a second time the pupils should, when sufficiently advanced, prepare themselves by private reading for their *vivâ voce* lesson; extracts from standard authors should be read to them; and this higher instruction should be followed by compositions, the pupils taking passages from the familiar Manual as headings to their essays.

H. A.

Nassau House, Barnes.

N.B. — This translation is made and published by special permission.

CONTENTS.

ANCIENT HISTORY.

ASIA.

	Page
Egyptians	1
Indians	2
Phœnicians	ib.
Assyrians and Babylonians	3
Medes	4
Persians	ib.

EUROPE.

Greeks	5
Romans	9
Invasions of the Barbarians	14

MIDDLE AGES.

I. ARABS, FRANKS, NORMANS.

Justinian	16
Arabs	ib.
Franks	17
Normans	18
Feudal system	19

II. CRUSADES.

Papacy	21
France and England	23
Spain	24
Germany and Italy	ib.
Influence of the Crusades	25

III. FROM THE CRUSADES TO THE REFORMATION. — DECADENCE OF FEUDALISM.

Germany and Italy	27
Switzerland	28
The North	29
Turks	ib.
Slaves	31
France and England	32
Burgundy	33
Spain and Portugal	34
Italian Wars	35

MODERN HISTORY.

I. Reformation.—Religious Wars.—Absolute Rule.

	Page
Reformers	40
Elizabeth	41
Philip II.	42
Henry IV.	43
Maurice	ib.
Thirty Years' War	44
Gustavus Adolphus	45
Richelieu	ib.
Cromwell	46

II. Age of Louis XIV.

	Page
William III.	48
War of Succession in England	49
War of the Spanish Succession	ib.
European Colonies	50
Eastern Europe	51

III. Eighteenth Century.

	Page
Peter the Great	52
Alberoni	ib.
Prussia	53
Frederick II.	54
Maria Theresa	ib.
Catherine II.	55
European Colonies	ib.
United States	56
Washington	ib.
France	ib.

IV. French Revolution.

	Page
Napoléon Bonaparte	58
Congress of Vienna	60

V. Nineteenth Century.

	Page
Emancipation of the Greeks	61
Emancipation of the Colonies of America	62
Revolutions of 1830	ib.
Revolutions of 1848	63
War in the East	64

	Page
Chronological Table	65

MANUAL

OF

GENERAL HISTORY.

ANCIENT HISTORY.

ASIA.

THE fertile banks of the Nile, the Ganges, the Euphrates, the Tigris and the Oxus were the places where men first established themselves and founded different states, about 2200 B.C. In all these places there was a ruling caste or tribe, that of the *priests*, which reserved to itself the control of religion and the chief authority (*Theocracy*). These *priests*, though known under various names, Brahmins, Chaldæans, Magi, &c., seem to belong to the same race of men.

Egypt, of which the earliest mentioned *Egyp-*
king is **MENES**, was divided into several *tions.*

B

small states. Sesostris [1500] united most of these. Psammeticus [656] placed the Egyptians in communication with the neighbouring peoples. This country was conquered, under Psammenitus, by Cambyses, king of Persia [525].—The principal divinities of the Egyptians were Ammon, Osiris and Iris.

Indians. The Indians, whose civilisation was as ancient as that of the Egyptians, were, like them, divided into several castes, the chief of which was that of the Brahmins. Their legislator was Menu and their language the *Sanscrit,* the most ancient of all the Indo-European languages. Their principal divinities were Brahma, Vishnu and Siva, the powers of creation, preservation and destruction.

Phœnicians. Among the peoples of the Shemetic race are to be distinguished the Jews, Arabs and Phœnicians. The Phœnicians settled on the eastern shore of the Mediterranean, and became the most commercial people of antiquity. They founded colonies and dépôts in most of the coun-

tries between the Atlantic Ocean and
India. Their most important colony was
Carthage, on the coast of Africa, which
became a very powerful state.—The Phœnicians were conquered by the Assyrians,
and afterwards by the Persians.

The countries between the Tigris and *Assy-*
Euphrates seem to have formed in the *rians*
and
earliest ages a Chaldæan empire of which *Baby-*
lonians.
Babylon was the centre until 1273 B.C.,
at which epoch the Assyrians established
themselves there and gained the supremacy. Under the reign of PHUL [*about*
750] the Medes freed themselves from the
Assyrian yoke, and Nabonassar founded
at Babylon a new Chaldæan dynasty.

Still the Assyrians prevailed under
TIGLATH PILESER, and above all under SHAL-
MANESER [729]. They reduced Damascus,
the kingdom of Israel, Syria and Babylon;
and, under Sennacherib, endangered the
independence of Judah and of Egypt.

But, east of the Tigris, the Medes, who
had become formidable by their union
under one prince [Deioces, 656], although
checked for a time by the invasion of the

Scythians, formed an alliance, under the
reign of Cyaxares, with NABOPOLASSAR,
governor of Babylon, took Nineveh [606]
and put an end to the Assyrian empire.

Babylon, having thus recovered its independence, inherited the rights of Assyria
over the south-western provinces, and
under NEBUCHADNEZZAR [605] further extended its dominion by the conquest of
Tyre and the kingdom of Judah. Egypt,
too, succumbed for a time. The rule of
the Babylonians lasted until the taking
of their capital by Cyrus, king of Persia
[539].

Medes.   The Medes (*predominant tribe, the
Magi* — ZOROASTER) succeeded the Assyrians. Their empire comprehended the
countries situate between the Tigris and
the Indus ; they were reduced by Cyrus,
king of Persia.

Persians.   The Persians, whom CYRUS made independent [560], conquered successively
Media, Babylonia, Phœnicia and Lydia,
of which last named country Crœsus was
then king ;—in a word, all the countries
between the Indus and the Mediterranean. CAMBYSES, the second king,

added Egypt, and Darius organised, to a certain extent, this vast empire. After long wars with the Greeks the Persians were subjected, under the reign of Darius Codomanus, by Alexander, king of Macedonia [333].

EUROPE.

The races which compose the population of Europe are; the *Pelasgian* race in Greece and Italy, the *Germanic* race in Germany, the *Sclavonic* race in Russia, Poland, Bohemia, Hungary and the north of Turkey, and the *Keltic* race in the western part of Europe.—Some historians admit an *Iberian* race in Spain. History treats chiefly of the first two of these races.

Greeks.

Greece was first peopled by the Pelasgi, to which people the Hellenes probably belong. The *myths* of Cecrops, Danaus and Cadmus seem to indicate the intro-

duction of foreign elements (Egyptian
and Phœnician) into Greece.

It is difficult to say precisely what
historical value can be assigned to such
events as the Argonautic Expedition,
the War of Thebes and of Troy, and the
Return of the Heraclides. They belong
to what is termed the *heroic* period of
Greek history.

After this period Greece seems to have
been divided into a number of small republics. The Dorians, one of the principal of the Hellenic tribes, predominated
in Sparta, Argos, Corinth and throughout nearly the whole of the Peloponnesus. The Ionians, the other principal
tribe, inhabited Athens, most of the
colonies of Asia Minor and the islands
of the Archipelago. The other tribes
were the Achæans, who peopled the
North of the Peloponnesus, and the Æo-
lians of Hellas proper and the coast of
Asia Minor. The *Amphictyonic Council,*
the oracles and the national games served
to unite the several states of Greece.
The first among these states were Sparta
[LYCURGUS, 880] and Athens [SOLON, 594].

The Greeks of Asia Minor, aided by
the Greeks of Europe, having revolted
[501] against King Darius the Persians
attempted the conquest of Greece; but
they were repulsed by the Athenians,
under MILTIADES [490]. Ten years later
the Spartans, under LEONIDAS and PAU-
SANIAS, and the Athenians, under THE-
MISTOCLES and ARISTIDES, baffled a second
attempt directed by Xerxes, king of
Persia [480 and 479]; and afterwards
Athens, whose powerful fleet was con-
fided to CIMON, forced the Persians to
recognise the independence of the Greek
colonies [449].

From this time the Athenians, the
most civilised of all the Greeks, under
PERICLES [444], arrogated to themselves
the supremacy over all the other republics and excited a long war, called
the *Peloponnesian War* [431]. They
failed in an expedition against Sicily
[415], and, notwithstanding the efforts
of ALCIBIADES, Athens was reduced and
taken by the Spartan LYSANDER [404].

The Spartans, who had now the chief
sway, carried on, under AGESILAUS, the

war against Persia. But the Theban
EPAMINONDAS reduced their power [371].
During his lifetime Thebes was supreme
among the Greek states.

Shortly afterwards the *Sacred War*
[356] gave Philip of Macedonia an op-
portunity of interfering in the affairs of
the Greeks whom he conquered [338],
forcing them to acknowledge him as their
ruler. His son ALEXANDER *the Great* reduced Asia as far as to the Indus. His
empire succeeded that of the Persians.
After the death of this conqueror [323]
his dominions were divided into three
monarchies, that of Egypt under the
PTOLEMIES, that of Syria under the SE-
LEUCIDÆ, and that of Macedonia.

The new Egyptian monarchy rose to
great fame on account of the centralis-
ation of commerce at Alexandria and
the encouragement given to science by
the Ptolemies.

Syria soon lost several provinces,
which became independent states. The
Parthians, under the ARSACIDÆ, founded
[256] a kingdom between the Tigris and
Indus which lasted till 226 A.D., when

ARDSHIR founded the second Persian empire (*dynasty of the* SASSANIDÆ).

Macedonia, which succumbed to the descendants of ANTIGONUS, was instrumental in causing the dowfall of Greece, which was weakened by the rivalry of the *Achœan* and *Ætolian leagues.*

All the Hellenic states were successively conquered by the Romans.

ROMANS.

ITALY was anciently occupied by the Etruscans, the Sabines, the Latins and the Siculi. The coasts of southern Italy (Magna Græcia) and the eastern part of Sicily were peopled by Greek colonies; their principal towns were Cumæ, Tarentum and Syracuse.

According to tradition Rome, founded B. C. 753, had at first seven kings, viz. ROMULUS, NUMA POMPILIUS, TULLUS HOSTILIUS, ANCUS MARCIUS, TARQUINIUS PRISCUS, SERVIUS TULLIUS, and TARQUINIUS SUPERBUS. Under the reign of the last mentioned king BRUTUS is said to have abolished the monarchical system at Rome [509]. After

the expulsion of the Tarquins the Roman
Republic, governed by two *consuls* who
were elected yearly, was agitated by those
quarrels between the Patricians and
Plebeians which led to the institution of
tribunes of the people, the war of CORIO-
LANUS and the creation of *decemvirs* who
were appointed to furnish the Romans
with laws [450]. At last, after a struggle of two centuries, public appointments
were equally accessible to all the Roman
citizens. During these internal agitations the Romans had successively possessed themselves of all the several states
of Latium, and under CAMILLUS they
began the conquest of Etruria, when
they were arrested by the terrible invasion of the Gauls who burned Rome
[389]. Rome, rebuilt by Camillus after
the departure of the Gauls, regained its
sway over the neighbouring peoples and
reduced the Samnites after a war which
raged throughout Italy [343–290]. The
Tarentines called Pyrrhus, king of Epi-
rus, to their aid, but the Romans drove
him from Italy and completed the conquest of Magna Græcia.

Having become masters of the whole
of the peninsula the Romans met with
the Carthaginians in Sicily, and after
three dangerous wars, called *Punic Wars*,
succeeded in annihilating that commercial republic which had predominated in
the western part of the Mediterranean.
In the first war [264] the Roman
REGULUS was defeated and taken prisoner,
but at its close the Romans had conquered
half of Sicily. Their ally HIERON, king
of Syracuse, possessed the rest. Some
years after they took Sardinia [237] and
reduced Cisalpine Gaul [222] and Illyria.
In the second Punic war HANNIBAL [219],
the most formidable enemy of Rome, re-
peatedly defeated the Romans, when
SCIPIO *Africanus*, having taken the greater
part of Spain from the Carthaginians and
invaded Africa, forced upon Carthage a
humiliating peace [202].

The Romans now turned their arms
against the monarchies formed by the
partition of the empire of Alexander the
Great. They conquered the kings of
Macedonia [197] and Syria [190].
ÆMILIUS PAULUS reduced the Macedo-

nians [168]; and while Scipio Æmilianus
completed the conquest of Spain and
destroyed Carthage, Mummius possessed
himself of Corinth and the rest of Greece
[146].

After the Gracchi had failed in their
attempts to bring about a reform, the
Romans, under Marius, wrested Numidia
from Jugurtha and checked the invasion
of the Cimri [102]. A little later
(although the republic had been weakened
by the *Social War*, the revolt of the
slaves headed by Spartacus, and the
civil wars headed by Marius and Sylla)
[80], Pompey defeated Mithridates, king
of Pontus, and added the kingdom of
Syria to the empire. Pompey, Crassus,
and Cæsar exercised together a predominant influence in the state (first *triumvirate*), until Cæsar, having conquered
Gaul, defeated Pompey and the faction
of the senate [48], and changed the
ancient government into a military monarchy, the chiefs of which were called
Cæsars or emperors.

Cæsar was assassinated ; but the re-
publican party having been suppressed

by the second triumvirate, Augustus,
Cæsar's heir, vanquished his rival Mark
Antony [30] and made Egypt a Roman
province. The Romans now possessed
all the countries around the Mediterranean, which served to unite all the
divisions of their empire.—The age of
Augustus was the golden age of Roman
literature. — In his reign Christ was
born.

The immediate successors of Augustus
made themselves odious by their tyranny
and licentiousness; but Vespasian [A. D.
69] upheld the imperial authority. His
son Titus destroyed Jerusalem and dis-
persed the Jews [70]. Agricola, Domi-
tian's general, conquered the southern
part of Great Britain.

Trajan, Hadrian, Antoninus, and Marcus
Aurelius [98–180] protected the Roman
territory against the Parthians and
Germans, and added to it Dacia and
Mesopotamia. But under their successors, who were raised to the throne
by the soldiery, the empire fell into
decadence. Diocletian [284], for the
better administration of government,

divided it into four parts. CONSTANTINE *the Great* [306] reunited these parts and established christianity. At last, after the death of THEODOSIUS [A. D. 395], two empires were definitely formed, that of the East under ARCADIUS, and that of the West under HONORIUS.

Inva-
sions of
the Bar-
barians.

The Germans, who had hitherto been contented to intrude upon the border countries, invaded the Empire of the West at the beginning of the Vth century and settled there.

The Alani, the Suevi, and the Vandals, passed into Spain, and the latter, under GENSERIC, went over to Africa.— The Visigoths, under ALARIC and ATHAULF, established themselves in Spain and the south of Gaul.—The Franks and the Burgundians occupied the north and east of Gaul.—The Angles and Saxons settled in Great Britain [449].

The terrible invasion, under Attila [450], of the Huns, an Asiatic race, did not alter the respective positions of these peoples. They all successively embraced Christianity.

ODOACER put an end to the Western Empire [476]. After him the Ostrogoths, under THEODORIC *the Great*, entered Italy [493]; but being driven out by Justinian, emperor of the East, a part of them rejoined the Visigoths, who with their aid were enabled to complete the conquest of Spain.—The Lombards penetrated into Italy under ALBOIN [568] and settled there.

MIDDLE AGES.

I. ARABS, FRANKS, NORMANS.

Jus-tinian. THE empire of the East lasted much longer than that of the West; and even under JUSTINIAN [527] his general BELISARIUS repulsed the Persians and Bulgarians, and recovered Africa from the Vandals. The same general and NARSES wrested Italy from the Ostrogoths, while TRIBONIAN prepared the *CORPUS JURIS* (*Codex, Pandectæ*). Justinian's successors were less successful against the Arabs.

Arabs. Converted to a new religion by MAHOMET [622], the Arabs extended their power under the khalifs, who succeeded their prophet in Syria, Egypt, and Asia Minor. They overthrew the new empire of Persia, and, advancing in another direction along the northern coast of Africa, took Spain from the Goths [711], a part of whom, however, remained independent

in Asturia. — During several centuries
the Arabs were the most civilised and
prosperous of nations. From their dominions were formed in later times the
three khalifats of Bagdad, Cordova and
Egypt.

The Arabs were arrested in their con-. *Franks.*
quests in the West by the Franks. From
the time of Clovis [481] this nation,
united to the Burgundians, had been
engaged in the conquest of Gaul to the
Pyrenees. It acquired its greatest de-
velopment under Charlemagne [800].
Through his victories over the Saxons
Charlemagne introduced Christianity into
Germany. He destroyed the kingdom
of the Lombards in Italy, and united
under his rule France, Germany to the
Elbe, the north of Italy, and Spain to
the Ebro. The rest of Italy was divided
between the Greeks, the Saracens and
the dukes of Beneventum. — From the
vast empire of Charlemagne were formed
[843] Lotharingia, France and Germany,
which were exposed to the invasions of
the Slaves, the Magyars (a people ori-

c

ginally inhabiting the Ural mountains) and the Normans. — The empire of Lotharingia merged into that of Germany. In France HUGH CAPET dethroned the last of the Carlovingians [987]. The Germans had chosen ARNULF for their king [887]. Among the successors of Arnulf were HENRY *the Fowler* and his son OTTO I. the Great [936] who checked the ravages of the Slaves, while the Magyars were forced to settle in Hungary, where they became the ruling people. Otto conquered also the north of Italy, and took the title of *Emperor*.

Normans. Taking advantage of the feebleness of the successors of Charlemagne the peoples of the North, generally called Northmen, invaded incessantly France, the Low Countries, and especially England. ALFRED the Great [871] succeeded in chasing them from England, but they returned under their king CANUTE [1014].

One of these bands of Normans established itself in the north of France (*Normandy*) under ROLLO [912] and embraced Christianity. A duke of this nation, WILLIAM I. *the Conqueror*, gained possession of England [1066] and divided the land among his Norman followers, who became the aristocracy of the country. Some years earlier ROBERT GUISCARD, another Norman, took southern Italy from the emperors of Constantinople, and founded the kingdom of Naples, which took the name of the *two Sicilies* when the Normans took Sicily from the Arabs.

About the year 1000 BOLESLAUS founded the kingdom of Poland and STEPHEN that of Hungary.

Feudalism prevailed in the empire of Charlemagne and in those countries which, like Naples, England and Palestine, received it to a greater or less degree from that empire.

Feudal system.

After the German conquests the soil remained *allodial* property, or entered into the domain of princes who yielded part of it to their clients as fiefs. Soon [*towards* 900] these fiefs began to become hereditary. On the other hand, on account of the weakness of the Carlovingians, the ravages of the Normans, Slaves and Magyars, and the violence of the *counts* and *dukes* who aimed at independence, the position of the allodial proprietors became insupportable. They applied to the powerful for protection, yielding to them their possessions, of which they themselves retained the use; these were called *arrear-fiefs*. Thus the feudal system may be described as a state of society depending upon a contract of assistance on the part of the lord and of fidelity on the part of the vassel. The feudal contract assured to the Suzerain, beyond forty days of military service, the rights of alienation, of confiscation and aids varying according to locality. The great vassals retained for a long time the rights of private war, of coining money, of administering justice throughout their domains, of exemption from tax, and independence of all tribunals save that of their *peers*.

II. Crusades.

The bishops of Rome, who called *Papacy.*
themselves successors of S. Peter, had,
from the earliest ages of our era, taken
the title of *pope* (father), and, especially
after the division of the Roman empire,
had sought to place themselves above
the other bishops of Christendom. With
the help of the Frankish kings they had
withdrawn themselves from subjection
to the emperors of Constantinople, and
governed independently the little state
of Ravenna [*about* 800] ; this was the
beginning of the *State of the Church.*
As the Greek bishops refused to acknowledge the supremacy of the popes a
schism took place, in the middle of the
11th century, which divided Christendom
into two Churches, the *Gréek* and the
Latin.

Henceforward the popes, taking advantage of the ignorance in which Europe was plunged, considerably increased
their authority. Gregory VII. [1073]
endeavoured to persuade the sovereigns

c 3

of Europe that, as *vicar of Christ*, he
was their superior ; he even excommuni-
cated the emperor of Germany, Henry IV. :
and thus Rome became again, in some
sort, the capital of the West.

1. URBAN II., one of the successors of
Gregory VII., caused to be preached in
the West, by PETER *the Hermit*, the *first
Crusade*, a holy war undertaken for the
purpose of rescuing Palestine from the
infidels. — GODFREY DE BOUILLON, who
commanded the crusaders, took Jerusalem, of which he was elected king
[1099].

2. The repeated attacks of the Turks,
a Tartar tribe that had conquered part
of the khalifat of Bagdad, made a *second
Crusade* necessary. LOUIS VII., king of
France, and KONRAD III., emperor of Germany, joined this crusade at the insti-
gation of S. BERNARD [1147] ; but their
expedition was fruitless.

3. SALADIN, sultan of Egypt, having
taken possession of Jerusalem, FRE-
DERIC (I.) *Barbarossa* of Germany,
PHILIPPE AUGUSTE of France, and RICHARD
(I.) *Cœur de Lion* of England undertook

a *third Crusade*, of which the only result was the taking of Acre [1190].

4. The *fourth Crusade* was directed against Constantinople [1202]; BALDWIN, count of Flanders, founded there the *Latin empire*, which lasted about sixty years.

5. ANDREW, king of Hungary, and WILLIAM I. count of Holland, engaged in a *fifth Crusade;* and after them the Emperor FREDERIC II., who recovered Jerusalem for a time by treaty [1227].

6 and 7. The *two last Crusades* [1248 and 1270], directed against Egypt and the state of Tunis by LOUIS IX. of France, were unsuccessful.

The kingly power was not firmly *France and England.* established in France until the reign of Philippe Auguste, who confiscated the Norman possessions of JOHN LACKLAND, and in whose reign INNOCENT III. ordered a Crusade against the Albigenses [Manichæans, Vaudois — 1208 — Tribunal of the *Inquisition*].

But in England after the reign of Henry II., the first of the Plantagenets,

c 4

the royal authority, already shaken by the struggle of this prince with the clergy [THOMAS À BECKET, 1170], was limited, under John, by the *Great Charter* [1214].

Spain.
The Spaniards, issuing from their retreats in the Asturias, recovered Leon and Castille from the Arabs. The ancient Gothic March formed the kingdom of Aragon. The Basques, who occupied the kingdom of Navarre, were nearly independent; and ALPHONSO I. made himself king of Portugal [1142].

Germany and Italy.
The constantly increasing power of the popes diminished that of the emperors of Germany. The great vassals declared themselves almost independent. The most powerful of them formed the *College of Electors:* these were the following;— the archbishops of Trèves, of Cologne and of Mayence, the king of Bohemia, the duke of Saxony, the count palatine of the Rhine, and the margrave of Brandenberg. These great vassals governed their states almost absolutely, only recognising in the emperor the power of executing the

measures upon which they had decided
in their common assemblies, or *diets*.
These measures concerned the interests
of the *empire*.

And as, since the time of Otto I., the
emperors persisted in asserting their rights
in Italy, the popes supported against
Frederic Barbarossa and his successors
the Lombard league, composed chiefly of
the republics of the north of Italy. The
partizans of the Emperor were called
Guelfs, and his adversaries Ghibelines.
And when, under Frederic II., the house
of *Hohenstaufen* had established itself in
the south of Italy the popes called to their
aid Charles of Anjou, brother of Louis
IX. of France. This prince conquered
the kingdom of Naples and Sicily [1266];
and although he lost Sicily after the
massacre called the *Sicilian Vespers*
[1282] he continued to be the chief stay
of the Guelfic party.

The influence of the Crusades was very
great in Europe. The kingly power was
augmented at the expense of the aristocracy and through the increasing importance of the *Commons*. The clergy

Influence of the Crusades.

lost in moral influence what they had gained in wealth and number (*Domini-cans, Franciscans*). The nobility were no more than the first of the free classes of the population, but their family names and armorial bearings kept them distinct. The disorders of the time, led to the institution of *chivalry*. In support of the Christians in the East orders, at once military and religious, arose : that of the *Hospitallers*, established successively at Rhodes and Malta ; the *Teutonic* order, who, later, settled in Prussia and Livonia; and the *Templars*. — Very many cities having obtained their freedom, either by revolt or by purchasing their liberty, immediately submitted themselves to the sovereign of the country, who in return granted them certain privileges, of which the right of making their own laws, bearing arms and regulating customs were the principal. In order to promote commerce and to protect their liberties several *leagues* were formed, as those of Lombardy, Flanders, the Rhine, and the *Hanseatic League* [1241], the most im- · portant of all, which embraced as many ·

as 70 cities. The Mediterranean route was opened to trade by the Christians. The republics of Pisa, Venice, and Genoa extended their commerce and soon became the dépôts of the eastern and western markets, and merchandise was conveyed into the different countries of Europe through the intervention of the confederate cities. — The learning of the Greeks and Arabs penetrated into the West, where several *universities* were founded, as those of Paris, Oxford, Cambridge, Salerno, Bologna, Padua, Salamanca and Coimbra.

III. FROM THE CRUSADES TO THE REFORMATION. — DECADENCE OF FEUDALISM.

In order to put an end to the anarchy which prevailed in Germany after the fall of the Hohenstaufen the electors chose RUDOLF of Hapsburg [1273], who followed a course very different to that of his predecessors. Retaining no claims in Italy save the title of *King of the Romans*, he sought to create for his family an independent hereditary state.

Germany and Italy.

With that view he conquered Austria, which had formed part of the kingdom of Bohemia, and thus became the founder of the *House of Austria*, which soon became so powerful that, after the extinction of the house of *Luxemberg*, the emperors were almost always chosen from its members. The successors of Rudolf exerted themselves in extending the heritage left to them.

Freed from its wars with the emperors, Italy became divided into a number of small states independent of each other. The maritime cities remained republics, while the rest were subject to sovereign princes. The most famous of the sovereign families of Italy were the VISCONTI and SFORZA (Milan), the GONZAGA (Mantua), the house of EST (Ferrara), and, eminently, the MEDICI (Florence), who, during the fifteenth century, distinguished themselves above the rest by their magnificence and their patronage of the arts and sciences.

Switzerland. Under ALBERT, a successor of Rudolf of Hapsburg, the members of the three *Swiss Leagues* (inhabiting Uri, Schwyz, and Unterwalden) revolted, and formed the three first cantons of the *Helvetian Confederation* [1307].

MARGARET, queen of Denmark, added *The North.* Norway and Sweden to her dominions [1397] by the *Union of Calmar;* but, as her successors favoured the Danes, discords ensued which led to the rupture of the union [1523] under CHRISTIERN II.

The house of Austria entered upon a *Turks.* crusade, the object of which was to check the inroads of the Turks who threatened Christendom. — The Seljuk Turks overthrew the temporal power of the khalifs of Bagdad [1038].—Another Turkish tribe, escaping the dominion of the Mongols under ZENGHIS KHAN, settled at the foot of Mount Olympus and entered the service of the sultans of Iconium. These Turks, called Ottomans, from OTHMAN their first *Sultan,* regained their independence and made Bursa their first capital [1326]. ORCHAN, Othman's successor, passed into Europe and established a body of troops called Janissaries, by whose aid MURAD I. and BAJAZET ex-

tended their power in Europe and Asia.
Although checked for a moment [1402]
by the Mongols, under TIMOUR THE LAME,
they pursued their conquests during the
fifteenth century. MURAD II. reduced
Asia Minor and the Slave tribes who
had established themselves in the Byzan-
tine empire. MAHOMET II. took Constantinople [1453] and put an end to the
Eastern Empire. He completed the conquest of Greece, and defeated the Tartar
tribes of the north of the Black Sea.
Under SOLEYMAN the Turks attained the
highest pitch of their glory: their dominion succeeded that of the Arabs in
Syria, Egypt, and the north of Africa.

When the news of the taking of Constantinople was spread, and, above all,
when it was known that Venice had con-
sented to pay tribute to the *Infidel*, and
that a Turkish fleet was ravaging the
coast of Italy, Europe was alarmed, and
the popes, of whom Pius II. was the
most zealous in the cause, preached a
crusade. GEORGE CASTRIOT (Scanderbeg),
JOHN HUNNYAD and MATTHIAS CORVINUS —

son of the latter and king of Hungary — were the true bulwarks of Christianity, and arrested the progress of the Turks. After this period the Turks alarmed Germany more than once, and twice laid siege to Venice; but these successes were but temporary, and Hungary remained the limit of their empire in Europe.

Among the Slavonic states Poland, *Slaves.* under the *Jagellons*, plays the most important part. In the fifteenth century it comprised Lithuania and Galicia, and disputed the dominion of eastern Prussia and Livonia with the Teutonic Order. — A little farther eastward the *czar* of Muscovy, IVAN III. [1462] rendered himself independent of the Tartars, and thus established in the Russian monarchy a rival to Poland. But in Germany the Slaves lost their nationality. JOHN ZISCA, during the Hussite wars, and GEORGE PODIEBRAD long defended Bohemia ; but, after the death of SIGISMOND [1437], this kingdom became one of the hereditary states of the house of Austria. •

France and England. We have seen how Germany and Italy were broken up into a number of little states; France, on the other hand, from the time of Philippe Auguste and Louis IX., acquired more and more unity. The kings of France, whose dominions increased considerably during the crusades, found in the commons a powerful support against the feudal lords. They had little to fear from the popes: when BONIFACE VIII. wished to excommunicate PHILIPPE-LE-BEL [*about* 1300] the whole realm united to resist the pope's pretensions. Then it was that *Etats-Généraux* (States General) were first convoked. Philip established pope Clement V. at Avignon and abolished the order of Knights Templars [1312].

After the death of CHARLES IV. [1328], the last of the *Capetians*, PHILIPPE of *Valois* and EDWARD III. of England disputed the crown of France; this was the origin of a war which lasted about a century. Edward III., having made an alliance with the Flemings, who were led by JACQUES ARTEVELD, and with a part of the Bretons, took Calais, and his son, the

Black Prince, gained great victories in the west of France. CHARLES V., aided by DUGUESCLIN [1364], checked the English for a time; but under his son, CHARLES VI., HENRY V. possessed himself of France as far the Loire, and caused himself to be crowned king at Paris [1419]. A young country maiden, JEANNE D'ARC, arrested the English before Orleans [1429] and saved France. CHARLES VII. gradually reconquered the provinces that had succumbed to the English, so that in 1453 our French possessions were reduced to Calais only.

During these wars the dukes of Burgundy had become so powerful that they rivalled sovereigns of the first rank. By marriage and conquest PHILIPPE-*le-Bon* added Franche-Comté and the southern provinces of the Netherlands to Burgundy. He forced JACQUELINE of Bavaria to surrender to him Holland, Zealand and Friesland [1428]. But Louis XI., king of France, who devoted himself to the ruin of the great vassals, destroyed this temporary power. Under him the

Burgundy.

D

Swiss defeated CHARLES *the Bold*, the last
duke of Burgundy, who died before
Nancy [1477], and Louis added the
duchy to his crown. The Netherlandish
provinces were united to Austria by MARY
of Burgundy's marriage with MAXIMILIAN.
Thus delivered from feudalism France
prepared for war with Italy.

England, distracted by the *Wars of the
Roses*, i, e. of the houses of York and
Lancaster, took no part in these events.
The accession of HENRY VII. [1485], the
first of the Tudors, restored the country
to comparative peace. This prince humiliated the English nobility.

Spain and Por- tugal.

Castile, Aragon and Portugal gained
ground so considerably after the Crusades
that, at the beginning of the XVth century, the kingdom of Granada was all
that remained to the Moors. The kingdoms of Castile and Aragon were united
by the marriage of FERDINAND *the Catholic*,
king of Aragon, with ISABELLA, heiress of
Castile [1469], so that Spain now formed
one state. These two sovereigns attacked
the Moors and took Granada in the same

year in which CHRISTOPHER COLUMBUS discovered for them America [1492]. Supported by the Inquisition, which TORQUEMADA had just newly organised, they weakened the power both of the aristocracy and the commons, and thus prepared a way for the absolute rule of Charles the Fifth.

Towards this epoch Portugal became one of the chief maritime powers. VASCO DE GAMA discovered the passage to the Indies by the Cape of Good Hope [1498], and ALBUQUERQUE founded the empire of the Portuguese in the East.

Until the time of LUDOVICO SFORZA the *Italian wars.* Italians had the prudence to avoid applying to foreign powers to settle their differences. But that prince, who had usurped the ducal crown of Milan, thought he could not sustain his authority without appealing to the French. Italy consequently became the theatre of a bloody war, which terminated in the loss of her liberty. CHARLES VIII. of France crossed into Italy [1494] and achieved the temporary conquest of the kingdom of Naples upon which he had claims. His successor, LOUIS XII., supported by CESARE BORGIA, who sought to create for himself a state in Romagna, rapidly reduced Milan and the kingdom of Naples [1499]. But the Neapolitans having called the Spaniards to their aid, Ferdinand the Catholic sent GONZALO DE CORDOVA to Naples, who conquered that country and added it to Spain [1503].

Pope JULIUS II., whose aim was to expel the foreigners from Italy, reunited the states of Cesare Borgia to the Holy See and humiliated the Venetians by the *League of Cambray* [1508]. Ferdinand the Catholic, Maximilian, emperor of Germany, and HENRY VIII. of England united with the pope in a *Holy League* [1511] against Louis XII. and drove the French from Italy. Nevertheless FRANCIS I., the successor of Louis XII., retook Milan [1516]; but he found he had to cope with a rival who was more powerful and clever than himself.

Maximilian of Austria had had by Mary of Burgundy a son called PHILIP *the Handsome*, who, by his marriage with

JOAN, daughter of Ferdinand and Isabella,
united the Netherlands and Castile under
one sceptre. Philip's reign was short.
CHARLES, the eldest of his sons, succeeded
him. At the death of his grandfather
Maximilian Charles was elected emperor
[1519] and was thus sovereign of the
Netherlands, Spain, and the kingdom of
the two Sicilies, and emperor of Germany.
Milan alone was wanting to him to unite
his vast dominions. Having formed an
alliance with Henry VIII. and Leo X.
he invaded Milan, beat Francis I. at
Pavia, took him prisoner [1525], and
did not set him free until he had fully
secured the conquered country.

The enfeebled Francis formed an alliance with SOLEYMAN and the protestants
of Germany; but Charles, notwithstanding the exhaustion of his wealth, repulsed
all his enemies. His brother FERDINAND,
who had just been crowned king of
Hungary, resisted the Turks before
Vienna [1529], and Charles defeated
them and drove them out of Germany.
In order to put an end to the piracies
of the Turks he favoured the establish-

ment of the knights of Rhodes at Malta,
and took possession of Tunis, the chief
stronghold of the pirates [1535].

The latter wars of Charles V. against
France were less fortunate, and he ab-
dicated [1556], leaving Germany to
his brother Ferdinand, and his other
states, Spain, Italy, and the Netherlands,
to his son PHILIP II.—Charles V. raised
the house of Austria to its highest
power: but what neither the Turks nor
France had been able to accomplish was
brought about by the REFORMATION, which
destroyed a preponderance that had been
dangerous to the other states of Europe.

MODERN HISTORY.

I. REFORMATION. — RELIGIOUS WARS. — ABSOLUTE RULE.

THE popes increased their power by all available means; but they at the same time so transformed the religion of Christ that it was scarcely recognisable. Such men as ALEXANDER (VI.) BORGIA had disgraced the pontifical throne by their shameful wickedness. The abuses introduced by the papacy into the Church were so great that the latter councils, particularly that of Constance, had already sought to find a remedy, and began by limiting the power of the pope.

But God ordained that the truth should not be extinguished. The faith was preserved among the Albigenses and the Waldenses at the time of the Crusades; among the Wiclifites of England and the Hussites of Bohemia. Commerce, too (which was rapidly extended after the discovery of America), the invention of printing, and the learning which the fugitive Greeks brought from Constantinople into the West,—were all powerful means of spreading new ideas.

Reformers. The need of reform was, moreover, so deeply felt that the preaching of a poor monk was sufficient to separate from the church of Rome most of the states of the North. LUTHER and MELANCHTHON were the first apostles of the Reformation in Germany [1517], and ZWINGLE in German Switzerland. Although at first defeated by Charles V., the protestants of Germany, headed by MAURICE of Saxony, forced the emperor to allow them liberty of conscience [peace of Augsburg, 1555].

Sweden embraced the reformed religion in 1527, almost at the same time when GUSTAVUS VASA delivered her from the yoke of the Danes. Denmark declared herself protestant in 1536, at about which date Henry VIII. began the *Anglican Reformation.* CALVIN [1535] and BEZA preached protestantism in the West, and, unsubdued by persecution, the reformed faith was introduced into the, western and eastern provinces of France, into Switzerland, the Netherlands, and, by KNOX, into Scotland.

In order to check this rapid progress Rome had recourse to an expedient which had served her in her dealings with the Albigenses. She armed the Roman Catholics of Southern Europe as for a holy war — a new crusade, — and instituted a new religious order, that of the *Jesuits* [founded by IGNATIUS LOYOLA, 1540], by which means she purposed to give unity to the *league*, and inspire it with the zeal necessary for its endurance. On the side of papacy were the emperor of Germany, the elector of Bavaria, the duke of Savoy, and, above all, Philip II. of Spain, who, through his fanaticism, the magnitude of his dominions, and the great wealth he drew from America, was at first the leading member of the *catholic league*. Rome was also supported by a powerful party in France headed by the Guise family.

At first the protestants rallied round *Eliza-beth.* ELIZABETH, queen of England [1558], as

did the Roman Catholics round Philip II.
A struggle began in Scotland against
MARY STUART, in which the protestants
had the advantage; the Queen of Scots
was defeated by her rival, and her fall
was a death-blow to catholicism in Scotland. The theatre of war was now
transported to France and the Netherlands, where the protestants were headed
by Admiral DE COLIGNY and WILLIAM OF
ORANGE.

Philip II. Philip II., confounding in the same
hatred the Calvinists and the Flemish
nobles whom he had wearied by his
tyranny, determined to try the force of
persecution. He established the inquisition in the Netherlands, and sent thither
the duke of ALVA to execute his plans
of vengeance. In France the Guises and
CATHERINE de Medicis, unable to conquer
the Huguenots while under arms, attempted, on the eve of St. Bartholomew's
day [1572], and at a time of peace, to
massacre them all by treason. But all
these cruelties served only to stir up a
spirit of exasperation in the two coun-

tries. The Netherlands revolted, and, under William I., the northern provinces declared themselves independent [1579]. War was renewed in France by the protestants. The Catholic *league* was then organised and placed in connection with Spain by the monks and the Guises. Philip II., now [1580] master of Portugal, equipped a formidable fleet, the Armada, with which he thought to terminate the quarrel by one blow. His fleet was ruined. Aided by the queen of England, the protestants of France and the *politiques*, a sort of third party, placed **HENRY IV.** on the throne [1589]; but he was obliged to become a Roman catholic, in order to be acknowledged by the leaguers: the protestants, however, obtained of him the *Edict of Nantes* [1598], by which liberty of conscience was assured to them.

This prince, the first of the *Bourbons*, *Henry IV.* re-established peace in France and disarmed the *league*. He constantly supported the protestants in order to humble the overgrown power of Austria. **MAURICE** of Nassau was enabled to main- *Maurice.*

tain the integrity of the United Provinces against Spain, and even to monopolise her commerce with the East Indies. The Dutch replaced the Spanish and Portuguese in the Indies, and became for a time the principal commercial nation of Europe.

Thirty Years' War. The religious war had not, up to this time, much agitated Germany, and the Reformation pursued there its march. Protestantism had made way in Austria, Hungary, and Bavaria. It was in Germany that Rome, whose projects had failed elsewhere, made a last effort. After the death of Philip II. she centred all her hopes in the emperor FERDINAND II., the pupil of the Jesuits. This latter period of the religious wars has been called the *Thirty Years' War* [1618— 1648].

At the beginning of the war the protestants were worsted, for England and France (governed by James I. and the regent Marie de Medicis) kept themselves almost aloof from the struggle. The Elector Palatine was driven from his dominions, and Denmark was forced

to conclude a disgraceful peace. WALLEN-
STEIN and TILLY, generals of the catholic
league, reduced almost the whole of
Germany.

The protestants found a champion in *Gustavus*
GUSTAVUS ADOLPHUS, king of Sweden. In *Adol-*
phus.
less than two years [1630—1632] he
delivered the north of Germany, which
rallied around him, defeated the catholic
generals, reduced the electorates of Trèves
and Mayence, retook the Palatinate and
invaded Bavaria. Death arrested his
conquests, but France took his place
against Austria. From this period the
war became almost entirely political.

LOUIS XIII., son of Henry IV., chose for *Riche-*
his minister Cardinal RICHELIEU [1625]. *lieu.*
This prelate began his career by stifling
in France every seed of discord; he suppressed the power of the nobles, and
made the king's authority absolute. Then,
full of confidence, he joined the enemies
of Austria. Taking into his pay the
armies of Sweden, he kept Austria at bay
and attacked the Spanish in Flanders and
Italy. He stirred up a rebellion in
Catalonia, and encouraged the revolt in

.Portugal by which that country recovered its independénce, 1640. At last,
after the Dutch, under TROMP, had ruined
the Spanish fleet in the *Downs* [1639],
and CONDÉ and TURENNE their land forces,
the exhausted house of Austria determined upon peace. Rome recognised the
impossibility of ruining protestantism.
— At the *Peace of Westphalia* [1648] the
limits of the joint states of Europe
were arranged much as they are at pre-
sent, save that Sweden possessed almost
all the coasts of the Baltic sea, while
Naples, Milan, and Belgium were under
the sway of Spain : the subsequent wars
were no longer *religious* wars, but took
place because such or such sovereign
sought to disturb what was from that
time called the *balance of power*.

Crom-
well.

England did not take part in the *Thirty
Years' War*. JAMES I. *Stuart*, who, after
the death of Elizabeth, united the crowns
of England and Scotland, and his son
CHARLES I. attempted to maintain the
absolute power of the *Tudors;* but the
Puritans, a religious sect who considered

the Anglican reformation incomplete, acting in concert with the parliament, revolted against Charles I. CROMWELL, who placed himself at the head of the insurgents, defeated the king, whom he caused to be beheaded [1649], and was appointed *Lord Protector* of England. He prepared the way for the great maritime power of this country, which he restored to the rank she had held under Elizabeth.

II. AGE OF LOUIS XIV.

France governed by LOUIS XIV. [1643–1715], united and strong after the trifling civil war of the *Fronde* (MAZARIN), was the first to attempt to upset the balance of power in Europe. Louis XIV., supported by his two ministers COLBERT and LOUVOIS, took French Flanders from the Spanish [1668]. Holland, finding herself menaced, formed an alliance with Spain, and became the centre of the party opposed to France, whose preponderance succeeded that of Austria. Louis XIV. gained to his side CHARLES II., who had

recovered the throne of England after
Cromwell's death, and invaded Holland
[1672]. Two great men frustrated his
attempts. DE RUYTER defeated the com-
bined fleets of England and France; while
William WILLIAM III. of Orange, who was raised
III. to the stadholderat in spite of the DE
WITTS, commanded the land forces, and
succeeded in detaching England from the
French alliance and opposed Germany
and Denmark to Louis XIV. The peace
of Nimeguen [1678] decided nothing.
Holland remained as she was, but France
gained Franche-Comté.—We have now
reached the most brilliant period of the
reign of Louis XIV. He possesses himself of Strasburg, interferes in the affairs
of the empire, ill-treats Genoa, humiliates
the pope, and bombards Algiers. In
order to complete in every way the unity
of France, he caused his clergy [1682] to
define the liberties of the *Gallican Church*,
and revoked the edict of Nantes [1685].
The persecuted protestants left France
in great numbers and joined her enemies.
From this time forward the power of
Louis XIV. gradually decreased.

In their hatred of Romanism, which *War of Succession in England.* the Stuarts attempted to introduce, the English expelled JAMES II. and invited William of Orange to take his place [1688]. The king of France, who wished to restore James, found England, the Empire, Holland, Spain and Savoy opposed to him. James failed in an attempt made in Ireland [1690], and Louis lost his fleet off La Hogue [1692], but his generals LUXEMBOURG and CATINAT resisted the efforts of the allied land forces. France was able to preserve her former conquests, but she recognised William III. as king at the treaty of Ryswyk [1697].

The Spanish branch of the house of *War of the Spanish Succession.* Austria became extinct in the person of Charles II.; and that sovereign having chosen for his successor Philip V., grandson of Louis XIV. [1700], the house of Bourbon occupied the throne of Spain. This was the cause of what is called the *War of the Spanish Succession.* Louis XIV., troubled at home by the insurrection of the *Camisards* (protestants inhabiting the Cevennes), suffered many

reverses abroad. The English general
MARLBOROUGH and Prince EUGENE of Savoy,
who commanded for Austria, beat the
French on several occasions. But the
Archduke CHARLES of Austria, the rival
of Philip V., having become emperor, the
allies feared to raise the house of Austria
too high by maintaining longer her cause.
A victory gained by Marshal VILLARS
led to peace [treaties of Utrecht and
Rastadt, 1713 and 1714]. France preserved her former limits; the house of
Bourbon continued to reign in Spain;
Belgium, Naples, Sicily and Milan were
transferred to Austria; and England
kept Gibraltar, which she had taken
during the war.

Euro-
pean
colonies.

Notwithstanding these wars the three
principal maritime powers, England,
Holland and France, spread themselves
beyond Europe. The Dutch formed
settlements on the coasts of Hindostan,
but especially in the Eastern Archipelago,
and colonised the Cape and Surinam.
They were even masters for a time of the
Portuguese colonies of Brazil.— The
English, whose maritime power steadily

increased, settled in North America and the Antilles, at Bombay and Madras. In 1702 the union of the two East Indian *companies* tended to develope their power in the East. The French occupied Canada and some of the Antilles, and formed settlements at Cayenne, Senegal and Pondicherry.

The crown of Hungary became heredi- *Eastern* tary in the house of Austria.—The Turks *Europe.* appeared once more before Vienna [1683]; but SOBIESKI, king of Poland, raised the siege, and prince Eugene forced them to return within their own territories [1699].

III. EIGHTEENTH CENTURY.

From the time of Gustavus Adolphus Sweden occupied the first rank among the states of the north. Supported by her alliance with France, she had retained Pomerania in Germany, conquered Livonia and Esthonia, and resisted Denmark, Poland and Russia; but at the beginning of the XVIIIth century she was obliged to yield to the preponderance of Russia. This Slavonic nation, cramped

at first by the Tartars and Poles, had
gradually extended itself at their ex-
Peter the   pense.   Under PETER I. *the Great* [1689
Great.   —1725] Russia became a European nation and predominated in the north.
Peter I., defeated at first by CHARLES XII.
of Sweden, finally succeeded in taking
from the Swedes two provinces of the
Baltic.   He founded S. Petersburg and
drove the Turks back to the Dniester and
the Tartars to the Caspian Sea.   These
successes enabled him to place his states
in communication with Europe and Asia,
and so to open hitherto barbarous regions
to the light of civilisation.

Alberoni.   Spain, under the ministry of cardinal
ALBERONI [1715], endeavoured to recover
what she had lost by the peace of Utrecht.
He aimed at once at depriving PHILIP OF
ORLEANS of the regency of France, at re-
placing in England the house of Hanover
[GEORGE I. 1714] by the Pretender (the
heir of the Stuarts), and at recovering the
Italian provinces.   He depended upon
the aid of Charles XII. of Sweden in
carrying out his projects, but they were

frustrated by the death of that king and the *quadruple alliance* of France, England, Holland and Austria. He was himself exiled.

Somewhat later, while Austria was engaged in an insignificant war in Poland, Spain recovered the kingdom of the two Sicilies, where she established DON CARLOS, son of Philip V. [1735] as sovereign. Thus the house of Bourbon reigned in France, Spain and Naples. Austria kept Milan, to which Tuscany was added as a fief of the empire, and Lorraine was promised to France. These are all the changes of any importance that took place under the feeble ministry of DE FLEURY in France and ROBERT WALPOLE in England.

The eighteenth century saw a new *Prussia.* protestant monarchy arise, that of Prussia, which soon counterpoised the influence of Austria in Germany. — In the time of Charles V. ALBERT, margrave of Brandenburg, joined to his states the possessions of the Teutonic Order (Oriental Prussia). His successors, particularly

the *Great Elector*, increased their territories, and in 1701 FREDERIC I. was
crowned king at Königsburg. His son
Frederic William I. and, eminently, FRE-

Fre- DERIC II. *the Great*, who succeeded the
derick II. latter in the year in which the Emperor CHARLES VI. left his hereditary

Maria possessions to his daughter MARIA THERESA
Theresa. [1740], considerably extended their territories. Although the leading powers
had promised to maintain the *Pragmatic
Sanction*, or the act confirming the imperial succession, all declared against
Austria save England and Holland, who
supported Maria Theresa and saved her
from losing her crown. Frederic succeeded in taking. Silesia; but elsewhere
the enemy was repulsed, and had not
Marshal SAXE triumphed in the Netherlands France might have lost her colonies.
These were confirmed to her by the
treaty of Aix la Chapelle [1748].

Maria Theresa, eager to recover Silesia,
gained to her side France (up to that
time the enemy of the house of Austria),
Russia, and Saxony, and recommenced
the war. This latter part of the Aus-

trian Succession War has been called the *Seven Years' War.* Frederic II. disarmed Saxony, and repulsed successively the French, Austrians and Prussians, while England, which was in league with Prussia, took Senegal, Canada and some of the Antilles from France. The treaties of Paris and Hubertsburg [1763] confirmed to the victors their conquests.

From this time Prussia, Austria and *Cathe-rine II.* Russia, now at peace, applied themselves to the spoliation of Poland. This country was dismembered in 1773 and the definite partition took place in 1795: Prussia had the grand duchy of Posen, Austria obtained Galicia, and Russia the rest. CATHERINE II. empress of Russia [1762—1796] acting in concert with JOSEPH II. of Austria, attacked Turkey. She extended her southern frontier to the Pruth, took the Crimea from the Turks and most of Finland from the Swedes.

The maritime preponderance of England allowed her to increase the number of her colonies. During the XVIIIth century she obtained almost all those of *Euro-pean colonies.*

3 4

France.   Lord CLIVE [1757] and WARREN HASTINGS established the English sway in India by the acquisition of Bengal, and ruined the French influence there.

United States.   But as England attempted to monopolise the trade of her colonies and to subject them to oppressive ⸀taxes those of America revolted.   WASHINGTON di-

Washington.   rected the military movements of the insurgents with success, and FRANKLIN went to Europe to seek allies.   France, Spain and Holland sided against England, which was compelled to acknowledge the independence of the United States by the treaty of Paris [1783].   Canada she retained.   India now became the chief object of her ambition, and long wars were sustained there against HYDER ALI, TIPPOO SAIB and the Mahrattas before her supremacy was recognised. — Captain Cook explored Oceania ; and towards the close of the century the English formed a settlement at Sidney in New Holland.

France.   Since the time of Louis XIV. France had ceased to play an important part in

Europe; her declining power was shown
in all the wars of the XVIIIth century.
Louis XV. rendered the kingly authority
despicable; deprived of all political power
by Richelieu, many of the nobles were
ruined by meddling in the monetary system introduced by Law [1717]; the phi-
losophers Voltaire, Rousseau, Diderot and
the Encyclopædists attacked religion and
threw contempt upon the clergy. The
national life was centred in the commons
(*tiers-état*) who imbibed the new ideas and
sought to emancipate themselves.—The
first proof of the change which was work-
ing in the public opinion was the expulsion of the Jesuits, who were successively
banished from all the Catholic states; the
abolition of their order was signed in
1773 by Pope Clement XIV.

Louis XVI. was unable to retard this
movement, and the French Revolution
began at the moment of the meeting of
the *States General* [1789].

IV. French Revolution.

The States General, under the name
of the *Assembly* (Mirabeau), and after-

wards the *Legislative Assembly*, diminished
the regal power. In 1792 the *National
Convention*, directed by ROBESPIERRE, proclaimed the French Republic (Committee
of Public Safety — Reign of Terror).
But the excesses committed by the republicans caused the French to adopt
another form of government called the
Directory [1795].

Austria and Prussia were alarmed, and
formed a coalition against France, under
the direction of the English government
(PITT), and supported by English money.
PICHEGRU and HOCHE, in the north, and
BONAPARTE, in Italy, triumphed over this
First Coalition. By the treaty of Campo
Formio [1797] Belgium was ceded to
France; Holland and Lombardy were re-
cognised as republics.

*Napo-
léon Bo-
naparte.*   After a short expedition in Egypt
Bonaparte returned and abolished the
Directory. Having been made *First
Consul* in 1799, he triumphed over the
Second Coalition, and, by the treaty of
Amiens [1802], forced England to re-
store the colonies she had taken from
Holland. Soon after Napoléon was

crowned *Emperor of the French and King
of Italy* [1804]. He now directed all
his force against England (*camp of Bou-
logne*); but the ruin of his fleet at Tra-
fálgar (NELSON) and the declaration of
war by Austria compelled him to turn
his arms against Germany [*Third Coalition*—Peace of Presburg, 1805]. Having
conquered the Austrians he was able to
dismember the German empire. Having
erected Bavaria and Wurtemburg into
kingdoms he united the minor states
under the name of the Rhine Confederation. Prussia was still more unfortunate
in the war of 1806 (*Fourth Coalition*),
terminated by the peace of Tilsit, 1807.
Napoléon took from her Westphalia, of
which he made a kingdom for his brother
JEROME. He also established his brother-
in-law MURAT at Naples, and his brother
JOSEPH at Madrid, notwithstanding the
resistance of the Spanish. Having
triumphed over the *Fifth Coalition* [1809]
he was master, directly or indirectly, of
France, Italy, Belgium, western Germany
as far as Hamburg, the Illyrian Provinces
and also of Holland, for the last-men-

tioned country which had been erected
into a kingdom under his brother Louis
[1806] was annexed to the Empire in
1810.

From this time forward Napoléon's
power gradually decreased. He lost an
army in Russia [1812]. The Spanish
and Portuguese, supported by the English
(Wellington), expelled the' French from
their country. The united forces of
Russia, Prussia, Sweden, England and
Austria (*Sixth Coalition*) beat the French
troops at Leipzig. The allied armies
poured into France at all quarters and
overwhelmed Napoléon [1814]. He attempted to recover his power [the *hundred
days*], but his defeat at Waterloo completed his ruin [1815].

*Congress
of Vi-
enna.*   The deputies of the different European
powers determined and guaranteed to
each other at the *Congress* of Vienna
[1815] the limits of their several states.
The Bourbons were re-established in
France, Spain and Naples [Louis XVIII.
Restoration — Ferdinand VII.]. It was
decided that Germany should form a *Con-*
federation whose deputies should consti-.

tute a *Diet* at Frankfort on the Maine,
the Austrian deputy presiding.—Belgium,
united to Holland, formed, under **WIL-
LIAM I.** of Orange, the kingdom of the
Netherlands. Poland, set free for a short
time by Napoléon, was ceded, as a distinct kingdom, to **ALEXANDER** of Russia.—
Norway, hitherto united to Denmark,
was bestowed upon **BERNADOTTE** of Sweden.
—England retained almost all the colonies
she had conquered during her wars with
Napoléon save Dutch Guyana and Java,
which were restored to the Netherlands.
Since this time her power has extended
itself in India.

V. NINETEENTH CENTURY.

After a struggle of seven years [1821–
1828] the Greeks regained their freedom,
and Turkey, by the armed interference
of England and France, was forced to
acknowledge their independence. This
struggle, together with the war she had
to sustain against Russia (terminated by
the peace of Adrianople), decided the
decadence of the Turkish empire.

*Eman-
cipation
of the
Greeks.*

Eman-cipation of the colonies of Ame-rica.

The Spanish provinces in America, isolated from their mother country during the wars of Napoléon, formed themselves into republics (Mexico, Guatimala, New Granada, Equador, Peru, Chili, La Plata and Paraguay) 1811–1824. Bolivar was the great leader of this war of independence. In 1822 Brazil separated herself from Portugal and formed herself into an empire under Pedro.

Revo-lutions of 1830.

The efforts of the republicans of Italy (*carbonari*) were forcibly stifled by the *Congress of Verona* [1822]. But in France Charles X., having violated the charter granted by Louis XVIII., was expelled with his family from France [July 1830], and the French chose for their king Louis Philippe of Orleans, who completed the conquest of Algeria (Abd-el-Kader). Belgium, supported by France, separated itself from Holland and formed a separate kingdom under Leopold I. Poland failed in a similar attempt, and Nicholas I. incorporated it with Russia. Spain saved its constitution by supporting Isabella II. and excluding Don Carlos. The Portuguese

dethroned Don Miguel and chose DONNA
MARIA [1834], daughter of the emperor
of Brazil, for their queen.

Europe was troubled in 1848 by a *Revolu-*
new revolutionary explosion, which was, *tions of*
1848.
however, of no long duration. The republic proclaimed in France lasted until
the *coup d'état* which re-established the
imperial government in the person of
NAPOLEON III. [1852].—It seemed for a
time that the different states of Germany
were on the point of becoming united
and acquiring constitutional liberties.
(*Parliament of Frankfort*). Austria,
threatened with dissolution by the revolt
of her Magyar and Italian subjects, recovered her unity under FRANCIS JOSEPH I.
[1849]. The Italian subjects of Austria,
although aided by CHARLES ALBERT, king
of Sardinia, were conquered, and the
quarrels of the Magyars (Kossuth and
Görgey), together with the armed interference of Russia, brought about the
suppression of the Hungarians.—On the
other hand Napoléon crushed the revolution at Rome against Pope PIUS IX.,
and Austria supported the other threat-

ened Italian governments. Democratical
ideas can only really be said to have
triumphed in Switzerland, for the *Son-
derbund* was defeated in 1847, and Neu-
chatel was freed from the rule of Prussia
(FREDERICK WILLIAM IV.) in 1848.

War in the East. Russia, which had kept aloof from
these agitations, attempted (NICHOLAS I.)
to extend her dominions at the expense
of Turkey ; but her armies were repulsed
and defeated by the allied forces of England and France. The accession of
ALEXANDER II. and the taking of Sebas-
topol put an end to the war [1855, *Congress of Paris*].

CHRONOLOGICAL TABLE.

ANCIENT HISTORY.

B. C.

2200. Menes.

1500. Sesostris.—Moses.

880. Lycurgus.

776. First Olympiad.

753. Rome founded.—Phul.

656. Psammetichus.—Deioces.

606. Nebuchadnezzar.—End of the new kingdom of Assyria.—Cyaxares.

594. Solon.

560. Cyrus.—End of the kingdom of Media.

538. Belshazzar.— End of the kingdom of Babylon.

525. Psammenitus.—Cambyses.

509. Tarquin.—Consuls at Rome.

490. Miltiades.—Darius.

480. Themistocles, Aristides, Leonidas, Pausanias.—Xerxes.

450. Cimon.—Decemvirs.

444. Supremacy of Athens.—Pericles.

431. Peloponnesian war.

404. Supremacy of Sparta.—Agesilaus.

389. Rome taken by the Gauls.—Camillus.

371. Supremacy of Thebes.—Epaminondas.

343. Samnite war.

336. Alexander the Great.

301. Antigonus.—Ptolemy.— Seleucus.

264. First Punic war.—Regulus.

F

B.C.

256   Parthians independent.

219. Second Punic war.— Hannibal.

202   Scipio Africanus.

168. End of the kingdom of Macedonia.—Æmilius Paulus.

146. Carthage and Corinth taken.

102   Invasion of the Cimbri.—Marius.

63.   End of the kingdom of Syria.—Pompey.

48.   Conquest of Gaul.—Cæsar.

30.   Augustus.—End of the kingdom of Egypt.

A.D.

70.   Jerusalem taken.—Vespasian.—Titus.

98.   Trajan.

226. New kingdom of Persia.—Ardshir.

284. Diocletian.

306. Constantine.

395. Theodosius.— Division of the Roman empire.— Honorius and Arcadius.

405. Invasion of the Barbarians.

429. Vandals in Africa.—Genserick.

449. Germanic hordes in Britain.—Attila.

476. End of the Empire of the West.—Odoacer.

MIDDLE AGES.

481. Franks in Gaul.—Clovis.

493. Ostrogoths in Italy.—Theodoric.

527. Justinian.—Belisarius.

568. Lombards in Italy.—Alboin.

622. Mahomet.—Hegira.

711. Arabs in Spain.

800. Charlemagne emperor of the West.

871. Alfred the Great.

A.D.

887. Arnulf.

912. Rollo.

936. Otto the Great.

987. Hugh Capet.

1000. Kingdoms of Poland and Hungary. — Boleslaus. — Stephen.

1066. William the Conqueror. — Robert Guiscard.

1073. Gregory. — Henry IV.

1099. First Crusade. — Godfrey de Bouillon.

1142. Kingdom of Portugal. — Alphonso I.

1147. Second Crusade. — Louis VII. — Konrad III.

1190. Third Crusade. — Philippe Auguste. — Richard Cœur de Lion. — Frederick Barbarossa.

1202. Fourth Crusade. — Latin Empire.

1208. Albigenses. — Innocent III. — Zenghis Khan.

1227. Fifth Crusade. — Frederic II.

1241. Hanseatic League.

1248. Sixth Crusade. — S. Louis.

1266. Charles of Anjou at Naples.

1270. Seventh Crusade.

1273. Rudolf of Hapsburg.

1282. Sicilian Vespers.

1300. Boniface VIII. — Philippe-le-Bel.

1308. Swiss Leagues.

1328. Philippe of Valois. — Edward III. — Murad (or Amurath) I.

1364. Charles V. — Duguesclin.

1397. Union of Kalmar. — Margaret. — Timour the Lame

1419. Henry V. at Paris. — Zisca.

1428. Jeanne d'Arc. — Philippe-le-Bon. — Jacqueline of Bavaria.

1453. Constantinople taken. — Mahomet II. — Matthias Corvinus. — Scanderbeg. — Podiebrad.

A D.
1462. Ivan III.
1469. Ferdinand and Isabella.
1477. Death of Charles-le-Téméraire (*i.e.* the Bold,.—
      Louis XI.—Maximilian of Austria.
1485. Henry VII. (Tudor).
1492. Discovery of America.—Christopher Columbus.
1498. Vasco de Gama doubles the Cape of Good Hope.
1508. League of Cambray.—Julius II.

* MODERN HISTORY.

1517. Luther.—Leon X.—Zwingle.
1519. Charles V. emperor.—Francis I.
1523. Gustavus Vasa.
1525. Charles V. takes Milan.—Soleyman.
1535. Calvin.—English reform.—Henry VIII.
1540. Ignatius Loyola.
1555. Peace of Augsburg.—Maurice of Saxony.
1556. Philip II.
1558. Elizabeth.—Mary Stuart.
1572. S. Bartholomew's Day.—Coligny.
1579. Union of Utrecht.—William of Orange.
1589. Henry IV.—Maurice of Nassau.
1598. Edict of Nantes.
1618. Thirty Years' War.—Ferdinand II.
1625. Richelieu.
1630. Gustavus Adolphus.—Wallenstein.
1640. Poland free.
1643. Louis XIV.—Mazarin.
1648. Peace of Westphalia.—Cromwell.

1672. Dutch war.—William III.
1678. Peace of Nimeguen.
1683. Sobieski saves Vienna.

A.D.

1685. Revocation of the Edict of Nantes.
1688. William III. of England.
1689. Peter the Great.
1697. Peace of Ryswyk. — Charles XII.
1700. Philip V. of Spain.
1701. Kingdom of Prussia. — Frederick I.
1713, 1714. } Peace of Utrecht and of Radstadt. — George I.

1715. Alberoni.
1735. Don Carlos at Naples.
1740. Maria Theresa. — Frederick II.
1748. Peace of Aix-la-Chapelle.
1757. Lord Clive in Hindostan.
1763. Peace of Paris and of Hubertsburg. — Catherine II.
1773. First Dismemberment of Poland. — Abolition of the Order of Jesuits.
1783. Republic of the United States. — Washington. — Pitt.

1789. French Revolution. — Mirabeau.
1792. French Republic. — Robespierre.
1795. Directory. — First Coalition.
1797. Treaty of Campo Formio.
1799. Second Coalition. — Bonaparte First Consul.
1802. Peace of Amiens.
1804. Napoléon emperor.
1805. Peace of Presburg, which terminates the third Coalition.
1807. Peace of Tilsit, which terminates the fourth Coalition.
1809. Fifth Coalition
1812. Russian campaign.
1813. Sixth Coalition. — Battle of Leipzig.
1814. The Allies enter France. — Wellington.

A.D.

1815. Battle of Waterloo.—Congress of Vienna.

1821. The Greeks declare themselves free.
1822. American republics.— Brazil independent.—
Congress of Verona.
1830. Taking of Algiers.—Louis Philippe I.—Leopold I.
1848. France a republic.
1852. Napoléon III. emperor.
1855. Congress of Paris, which terminates the war in the East.

THE END